The Sea House

'For my dad Jeff Cohen and his grandson Gabriel,
whom he never met but would have adored.'

Lucy Owen

'To my lovely Aunty Denny xxx'

Rebecca Harry

The Sea House

Lucy Owen

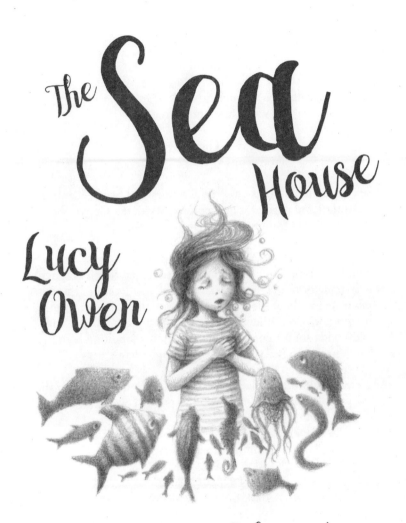

ILLUSTRATED BY Rebecca Harry

Firefly

First published in 2019
by Firefly Press
25 Gabalfa Road, Llandaff North, Cardiff, CF14 2JJ
www.fireflypress.co.uk

A CIP catalogue record of this book is available
from the British Library.

ISBN 9781910080825
ebook ISBN 9781910080832

*This book has been published with the support
of the Welsh Books Council.*

Typeset and designed by Claire Brisley.

Printed and bound by Pulsio, Sarl.

Contents

CHAPTER 1

Tears

Coral woke up. Her eyes snapped open in the darkness and she sat up, trying to work out where she was. She'd just had the same dream again. The one where she was with her parents and felt so close to them. They had all been back together, on a happy holiday, swimming in the sunshine, as if nothing had happened.

It was a shock to wake up back in her room. To remember again that her parents were gone. In the inky blackness of her bedroom, Coral had never felt more alone.

She was trying so hard to be brave for everyone. Her Aunt Trish and Uncle Jeff had moved in and were doing their best to look after her, and friends from school visited to try to cheer her up. But nothing could fill the huge hole in her heart. It didn't even seem worth coming out of her room when she didn't have to.

Coral had not let herself cry, not since the accident. She fought hard to keep her tears back, worried that if they began, they would never stop. But in the dark dead of night, after the hopeful bright island of her dream, she felt the grief surge inside her.

She gulped and gasped for air, almost drowning. Her heart was pounding. A sound like the ocean rushed and swirled in her head. Finally wave after wave of tears rolled down her cheeks, a sea of sorrow.

Coral couldn't hold back any more. She lay

back down on her bed, allowed her tears to flow free, and let herself be swept away.

Just before she cried herself to sleep, she closed her eyes and wished something would change. That something good would happen.

CHAPTER 2
Underwater

When she woke next, Coral didn't know what time it was, but she knew something was very, very different. Her long hair felt as if it was swaying. She turned her head a little and felt a ripple move through her hair, right to the very tips.

She tried to sit up. But that too was very, very different. It was a familiar feeling, but she couldn't think what it was. She felt slower, but at the same time lighter. It was almost as if she was under…

Coral's eyes widened.

UNDERWATER!

But that wasn't possible! How could she be underwater in her own bedroom? What had happened? How was she even breathing?

Coral exhaled and a stream of bubbles came out of her mouth.

She looked around. Her curtains were waving gently round her window, like long strands of yellow gingham seaweed. Apart from that, the room looked the same, though there was no doubt about it. It was underwater.

Out of the corner of her eye, at the far end of the room, Coral saw tiny blue flashes of light. Something very small was watching her, twinkling, sparkling and darting from side to side. The flashing grew faster and faster. Whatever-it-was spun around, dived down, shot up high, then whizzed back. Coral tried to follow it, but it was making her feel dizzy and a little bit seasick.

The zipping and the glittering stopped, directly in her line of sight. This glimmering little thing was looking straight at her.

It started to quiver, throwing shimmering jets of light around the bedroom like a sparkling diamond. Then it drew itself up and zoomed at top speed straight at her!

Coral froze. She braced herself for the worst.

Something was attacking her and she had no idea what to do. Her bedroom was underwater and now some sort of weird alien sea-being was whooshing right for her.

She sat still, screwed her eyes tight, tight shut and braced herself, ready to take whatever was coming.

She waited.

Nothing.

She waited a little longer.

Still nothing.

Coral didn't quite have the courage to open

her eyes. She could sense something very close. She felt slight stirrings in the water in front of her face. Somehow, she knew she didn't need to be afraid.

Slowly, she opened one eye, then the other. What she saw was totally and utterly unexpected.

CHAPTER 3
Fabulous

Hovering right in front of Coral's face was the tiniest, most exquisite little fish she had ever seen. Its excited, trembling body was a dark, velvety blue-black, covered with glittering spots that seemed to shimmer with a life of their own. Bright blue, pale blue, turquoise, silver, deep violet, all twitching and gleaming, illuminating her room like a disco ball. Coral was transfixed. She had never seen such a wonderful fish.

'I'm Fabulous!' said a sweet voice.

'Wow,' breathed Coral. 'Yes, you are!'

'No,' the fish giggled, like soft, tinkling bells. 'Fabulous. That's my name!'

As if to prove just how fabulous she was, she flipped a triple backwards somersault and blew a huge stream of bubbles, right at Coral.

'Fishes' kisses!' chuckled Fabulous. Her laughter was the first music in Coral's room for a long time. Coral giggled too as the bubbles popped against her face.

Seeing her smile, Fabulous launched into the somersault routine once again, whirled three times around Coral's head, tickled her nose with her tail fin, spun back around, blew another stream of splendid bubbles and took a bow.

'Definitely completely and utterly FABULOUS!' laughed Coral.

'That's me!' The little fish was clearly very pleased with herself. 'Right. You need to come and meet the gang!'

'You mean … there are more of you?'

It struck Coral that she was talking to a fish. And the fish was talking back. What was happening? But she didn't have time to think about it. Fabulous was on a mission.

'Come on, Coral, let's go! We've all been waiting for you. Everyone's going to be so excited! Especially Ramone.'

'Ramone? Who's Ramone?' asked Coral.

'You'll see, you'll see. We're going to have so much fun all of us, well, maybe not all…'

'What?'

'Ooops. Never mind, never mind. No need to worry about that now. Ramone will explain everything. Come on! It's going to take ages to get downstairs to see him because everybody is going to want to meet you.'

'They are? Why?'

This was all so much to take in.

Coral started to get out of bed and began to float up to the ceiling. She was lucky her parents had taught her to swim well! She gulped as happy memories of them filled her mind again. But Fabulous darted past, jolting her back into the present.

Floating above her bed, Coral looked down at her familiar, brightly striped duvet cover. This was unbelievable! She swam down, brought her feet under her and pushed back off the mattress, straight up to the ceiling. She brushed the yellow lampshade with her hand. Sea moss was already beginning to grow on it. Next, a swift dive back down to the floor to touch the green weed that was now covering most of the carpet. Coral swam around her room, skimming the walls, her desk, her wardrobe, kicking as fast as she could past posters, over her toys, her books, her skateboard, swimming right up to the door of her bedroom where Fabulous was waiting. The fish was looking at her with amusement, slightly puzzled at why swimming should be such a big deal.

'Seriously, Fabulous, you have no idea how weird it is to be swimming around your own bedroom – but it is SO, SO COOL!' Coral floated on her back, smiling.

'Okay … whatever you say…' said Fabulous, looking at her as if she was the one who was strange. 'But we have to go. Trust me, Coral, you're going to be doing a lot of swimming around your house from now on. Can you open the bedroom door? Oh and brace yourself, it is really busy out there!'

CHAPTER 4
Houseful

Swimming out of her bedroom, Coral could barely believe the scene before her. The landing was crammed with thousands of different sea creatures! There were fish everywhere she looked, some darting about, others swimming in huge shoals.

Coral could recognise many of them from her holidays. Her mother was mad about sea creatures and loved to teach her. There were angelfish, parrotfish, trumpetfish, lionfish, butterflyfish, triggerfish, trunkfish. There were barracudas, groupers, snappers, flounders, basses and wrasses, jacks and chubs. There were eels, jellyfish, snails, lobsters, shrimps, squids and starfish. It was as if her house had become a reef!

Looking down, Coral saw crabs scuttling along the patterned carpet. There were sandfish lying flat, trying to camouflage themselves in the shagpile. There was a rainbow of bright anemones, weird sea sponges and all different types of coral – some shaped like tubes of pasta, others like graceful, fine lace. There were even some that reminded her of giant brains!

Could this really be her home? She could still make out the bannisters and the stairs, the doors to the two other bedrooms and bathroom, but all around and in between was an explosion of sealife. It was her home, but it was a different world.

'Told you,' said Fabulous, obviously enjoying Coral's astonishment.

Coral saw a beautiful pair of pale pink seahorses bobbing slowly in front of them. She knew that seahorses are poor swimmers, but that they also have excellent eyesight.

'That's Dobbin and Swish,' whispered Fabulous. 'Thought it wouldn't take long for those two to spot you!'

The seahorses froze on the spot, and stared.

'It's her!' they exclaimed in unison, promptly linking tails and turning bright orange with excitement.

'Here we go,' muttered Fabulous. Coral felt very self-conscious.

A puffer fish turned when he saw the seahorses' spectacular colour change and noticed her. He puffed up on the spot, ballooning to resemble a small spiky rugby ball.

'Bubba the Puffa,' giggled Fabulous, 'always puffing!'

 Coral knew that when a puffer fish puffs, it's usually to scare away predators, so other fish always take notice.

And that's just what happened.

Like a ripple spreading through the water, Coral watched as shoal after shoal of fish, and all manner of strange and wonderful sea creatures, stopped to turn and stare at her. In just a few seconds the whole of the crowded, bustling upstairs landing had become completely silent and still. Thousands of pairs of eyes were fixed on her.

One little fish clearly loved being in the spotlight. Tiny in front of the multitude, Fabulous announced like a game show host, 'She's the one! The one we've all been waiting for! It is time! Put your fins, your tails, your tentacles together fooooooooor … CORRRRAAALLL!'

'Wait, wh–what's going on, Fabulous?!' Coral asked.

But nobody heard her, because the whole landing had erupted with frenzied cheering, whooping, bubble-blowing and fin-slapping.

'Make way, my fishy friends!' said Fabulous, enjoying herself no end. The crowd parted for them.

'Fabulous! Wait! Why is everyone looking at me?' Coral felt shyness creeping over her. It was strange just being out of her room, let alone having all these creatures staring at her.

'No time for questions now, Coral! Ramone will explain everything. You just swim with me and…' The little fish tilted slightly and squinted at her. 'And maybe try not to look so scared? Smile, wave, enjoy it!'

There was no choice. The little fish set a stately pace, revelling in the attention from the crowd. Coral swam behind, with an awkward lopsided grin on her face. As she passed, fish bowed reverently.

The over-excited Fabulous couldn't wait any longer. 'Come on! Let's pick up the pace! Ramone is waiting!'

Fabulous zoomed off down the stairs. Coral saw the bannisters were covered with a slimy, slippery sort of weed, and an idea popped into her head.

Coral loved skateboarding. She was pretty good at it too, having great balance. She hopped up on to the handrail and, imagining it was just like a skateboard, started to slide down it. This was fun! She gathered pace, faster and faster, swinging round the halfway post, skimming her way to the bottom and diving off into the hallway. Thousands of mesmerised sea creatures burst into applause once again. Coral smiled and took a little bow.

Scanning around her, Coral could see the

downstairs of her home had been transformed too. She swam through the hallway, trying to keep up with Fabulous, who had sped off into the living room. It was like swimming through an aquarium, but this was her house. A sea house!

*

Through the hordes of fish, Coral caught sight of something strange at the far end of the corridor. It was her kitchen door. Nothing odd about that. But it was firmly shut, and in Coral's house, the kitchen door was never closed. Her mother had always kept it wide open. 'The kitchen is the heart of a home,' she would say, 'and you should always keep your home and your heart open.'

Now though, the door was closed tight and – what was that? Coral narrowed her eyes. She thought she could see an eerie, greenish glow seeping out around the doorframe. She wasn't sure why, but Coral felt a shiver run down her spine.

CHAPTER 5

Ramone

*C*oral brushed off her uneasy feeling. Before she could even think about investigating, a throng of sea creatures propelled her into the living room.

Coral swam through the doorway. There were no other fish in here, apart from Fabulous, who was leading the way, spinning in circles with excitement. It was the same familiar lounge, except now there were barnacles on the bookshelves, long reeds swaying around the sofa, and seagrass covering the carpet. Her favourite photograph of her parents still hung on the wall. It had been taken on holiday. Coral stood in between them, holding their hands. Now algae had spread over the frame.

The other fish crowded in behind her and as soon as Fabulous was happy she had a good audience, she announced grandly, 'Coral, may I introduce you to...'

Fabulous paused dramatically.

'RAMONE!'

The crowd erupted with wild cheers and fin-slapping. Coral looked about her, but still couldn't see anything.

Then in the corner of the room, something began to turn around. Coral gasped when she realised what it was.

'HEEEEEYYYY CORRRRRAAAAALLLL!' boomed a deep lilting voice.

An enormous sea turtle started swimming across her living room towards her. Around his neck hung a mass of shell necklaces and he

wore a giant oyster shell on his head, pulled to the side like a rapper's cap.

'CORAAAAL!' said Ramone, coming to a stop in front of her. He looked searchingly into her eyes and Coral looked back into his. They were kind, wise, and extremely twinkly. The turtle burst into deep hearty laughter, clapping her a little too hard on the back with his fin.

'It is SOOOOOOOO good to see you, girl!

Ain't it, crew?'

The room exploded again with more crazy applause. Coral looked around her at the wondrous fish crammed into her living room and grinned. She couldn't help it.

'It really is amazing to meet you all,' said Coral, and she meant it. 'Although I'm not sure why my house has become a sea house?'

For a second, Coral thought Ramone looked troubled, but then he was laughing again.

'You weren't expecting us, hey, Coral, girl?'

He turned and boomed out to the crowd. 'We want to give you a proper Sea House welcome. Don't we, crew? Coral, do you like a bashment?'

'I'm sorry, a what?'

Fabulous giggled next to her. 'A bashment. It means a party. He may be nearly a hundred years old, but Ramone likes nothing better than a party!'

Coral couldn't believe that this super cool turtle was nearly a hundred years old!

'I love parties – I mean bashments!' Coral said, smiling.

'Then let's fling some tunes!'

The fish broke out into whooping once more. Coral was sure this party would be unlike any she'd ever been to before.

CHAPTER 6
Sea Spectacular

'It's show time!' said Fabulous, blowing a huge stream of bubbles and turning a backwards somersault.

More fish crowded into the room, over chairs, under coffee tables, squeezed onto bookshelves, hovering around the footstool, all leaving a space in front of the sofa for a watery stage area.

'Coral, Ramone, friends!' Fabulous was playing host. 'It is time for our Sea Spectacular. Put your fins, your tails, your tentacles together foooooooooooooooooooor … Otto and The Crevettes!'

A red octopus, who had cleverly camouflaged himself against the far wall, shot dramatically into the centre of the room. Hundreds upon hundreds of tiny bright pink shrimps broke out of the crowd. These were Otto's backing singers, the Crevettes.

The Caribbean beat was provided by a band of fish with black and white stripes on their heads and bodies, black and white spots on their fins. They looked as if they'd put on their best stage outfits. Each one was drumming its fins, thumping out a rhythm on pieces of furniture.

Otto launched into his song, half rapping, half singing, his tentacles rippling to the beat.

The Sea House Song

It's Coral, our Coral,
We know that she's the one.
Oh Coral, yeah Coral,
Shines bright as the sun.
She may not have gills,
She may not have fins,
But she's one of us,
We know she'll help us win.

In the Sea House, the Sea House,
It's where your best friends live.
In the Sea House, the Sea House,
All our love to give.
It's Coral, our Coral,
The one we're waiting for.
Oh Coral, yeah Coral,
The one we adore.
She so loves to sing,

She so loves to swim.
And she's one of us,
We know she'll help us win.

In the Sea House, the Sea House,
It's where your best friends live.
In the Sea House, the Sea House,
All our love to give.

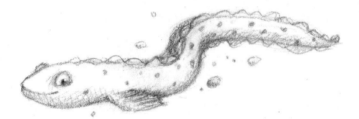

The Crevettes echoed the words, filling the room with sweet harmonies. Otto was busting some impressive dance moves. Ramone was popping his head and pumping his fins to the rhythm, his shell necklaces jangling together as he moved. The song was going down a storm.

'Let's hear it for Otto and The Crevettes!' exclaimed Fabulous, flipping wildly. 'And next up, I hope you're ready to party, because this is one eel who loves to dance! Let's hear it for Marvin "Hot Moves" MacKenzie!'

A pale grey eel covered in luminous orange spots snapped up in front of the sofa.

'Gimme a... He curled himself around, leaving a space between his head and tail.

'C!' shouted the fish loudly.

'Gimme an... Marvin pulled his tail end up to touch the top of his head.

'O!' chanted the crowd.

'Gimme a...' Marvin straightened his tail, and curved his head.

'R!'

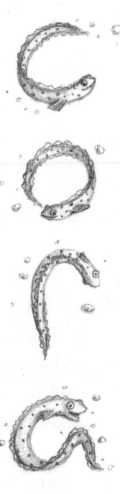

'Gimme an...' He contorted his body again.

'A!' yelled the audience, getting wilder as they worked out what he was spelling.

He straightened up to form his final letter.

'Gimme a...'

'L!'

'And what have you got?!'

'CORRRRALLLL!' everyone bellowed.

Coral blushed deeply.

Marvin launched into an extraordinary breakdance routine, spinning and sliding, sending the crowd into a frenzy.

'What's an eel's favourite dance?' Marvin asked, as he moonwalked backwards across the carpet.

'THE CONGA!' everyone yelled back.

'Well, what are we waiting for? Let's conga!' Marvin bowed low. 'Coral?'

Coral floated towards him.

'Hold on!' shouted Marvin. 'Everyone in a

line, here we go!'

The drumfish struck up a beat once more, and the conga began.

Coral hadn't had so much fun for a very long time. She was behind Marvin, Fabulous had pushed in behind her, next was Ramone, and thousands of other fish were all jumping into line.

Off they went, all shimmying and wiggling to the conga music.

Marvin led them out of the living room, along the hall, up the stairs, along the landing, around Coral's bedroom, then back down along the same route. The gigantic line was so long, one half of it was heading down the stairs as the other half was still heading up. Coral put out her hand and the fish gave it a friendly fin-slap as they passed.

As she bounced along behind Marvin, back through the hallway, Coral glanced towards the kitchen door. It was still tight shut and there was that same strange, unearthly light glowing around it. Coral once again felt a chill. Something was wrong, she knew it.

*

In the living room, the party was back in full swing. A troupe of starfish was elegantly forming one shape after another, like a kaleidoscope, to gasps of wonder. But Coral couldn't stop thinking about that ominous green glow from the kitchen. She had to find out what was in there. Even though Ramone and Fabulous hadn't said anything, somehow she sensed they wouldn't be happy about her going near the kitchen.

She glanced around. The creatures were all mesmerised by the starfishes.

'Ramone, I'm … I'm…'

Coral didn't want to be stopped. Something was drawing her to the kitchen and the green light. So she didn't finish the sentence.

The turtle didn't question her. He was swaying, watching the starfishes' display. 'Mmmmmmm … so beauuuutiful...' he murmured.

Coral swam to the back wall of the living room and edged along it, smiling and nodding innocently to any fish who glanced her way.

The hallway was empty. Everyone was in the living room watching the show. She looked at the kitchen door. The green glow seemed to be fading in and out, as if it were sending a signal, as if it were calling to her. She stared at the light.

'Coral…' She was sure she heard her name whispered through the water. 'Coral...'

She felt as if she were being pulled towards the kitchen. She couldn't stop herself swimming closer and closer.

'Coral...' Someone whispered her name

through the water again. The door began to open. 'Coral. Come to us. Closer, Coral...'

She was at the threshold now, the door opening wider and wider. Even though something deep inside her told her she shouldn't, Coral swam into the kitchen.

The door shut behind her.

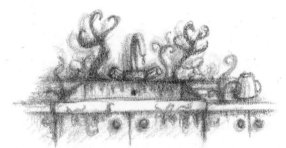

CHAPTER 7
The Kitchen

Coral blinked in the eerie light, trying to focus through the green haze. It was difficult to see, but she sensed she was not alone. She went to put her feet on the kitchen floor.

'Ouch!' Her foot touched something sharp. She heard cruel laughter.

She drew her knees up quickly and reached out to her mother's kitchen table for balance. Memories of happy family mealtimes flashed through her mind.

'Owwww!' Her hand was stung by something spiky this time. There was another ripple of cold sniggering. Who was that? Her heart beat quickly as she tried to work out what had happened to the room her mother had cherished.

As her eyes adjusted to the ethereal green light, Coral could see the wrecked kitchen. Once warm and welcoming, it was now cold and dark. It made her feel hopeless.

What had stung her? She looked and gasped. There were hundreds, maybe even thousands, all covered in black spikes – sea urchins!

Coral remembered being told they had spines to protect themselves, but these sea urchins seemed to enjoy hurting her.

She kicked back, swimming towards the door. This had been a bad, bad idea.

'Ohhhhhhhh, I don't think so,' said a chilling voice from the darkness.

'Who – who said that?' she stammered, turning round, her heart hammering in her chest.

'I must apologise,' the voice went on smoothly, 'for my urchin friends. No harm meant, I'm sure.'

Coral heard horrible laughter. Now she could see the urchins were everywhere, covering the floor, her kitchen table, mounting up over the units, piling high towards the ceiling, their spikes jutting out, waiting to strike. Fear lurched in her stomach, but she took a deep breath.

'I can't see you. Show yourself.'

The urchins mumbled and shifted. Then, at the end of the kitchen near the back door, Coral saw an enormous dark shape rise from the shadows. Propelled by what looked like giant wings, it moved gracefully but menacingly towards her. Its orange eyes burned on either side of its head.

Coral felt fear clutch at her again. A stingray. For some reason they had always terrified her. She had only seen one in an aquarium before. Closer and closer it came, staring at her with fiery eyes.

'I've been waiting for you to drop by,' the stingray drawled. 'I was so terribly sorry to hear about the death of your mother and father.'

Coral flinched. He moved closer still, inches from her face, staring deep into her eyes.

'What a tragedy. Still so young. And leaving you. Poor Coral,' he sneered.

Coral's body sagged. She felt so alone.

Reading her face, he continued. 'You try so hard to fight the sadness, don't you? But it's so hard, when there seems so little hope, with your parents gone forever.'

How did this beast know her darkest thoughts? Coral felt desperation well up in her.

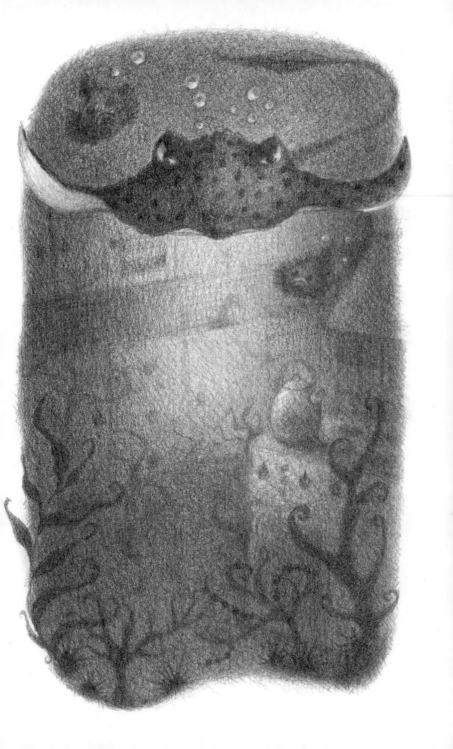

His words pierced her heart as sharply as if his poisonous tail were digging into her.

'Give into your grief. Stay in here with us, where nobody hopes for anything. Squadron Stonefish! Rocky! Edge!'

A troop of stonefish, who had been hiding behind the stingray, emerged from under his wings. They grinned at her, exposing grisly sets of sharp, pointed teeth.

'Join us, Coral,' breathed the stingray soothingly. 'Hide away with us. Why try to do anything? How can you be partying and enjoying yourself?'

Coral was in a trance, transfixed by the stingray. The green haze seemed to be closing in. The stingray's eyes burned brighter. He was right. She did want to escape from her pain. Why not stay in the dark where nobody hoped for anything or tried to have any fun?

CHAPTER 8
To the Rescue

A spark of blue light flashed past her, snapping her out of her trance. Coral shook her head. 'Fabulous?'

'Get out of here, Coral! They won't want to let you go! Swim to the door! GO!'

Coral made for the door, but the urchin army was on the rise, piling on top of each other to block her path. She reached through them and grasped the doorknob. Hanging onto it, she pulled as hard as she could, but the urchins were building their towers around her, making the door impossible to open.

Fabulous sheltered under her arm. 'You can do it, Coral, pull!'

She could feel their spikes now, grazing her arms, her legs. She glanced back and saw the venomous stingray poised to attack. The look in his eyes was enough to make her muster all her strength and give the door one final wrench.

She heard the crunch of spikes and saw piles of urchins crumble. As the stingray launched towards her, the door opened just enough for her to push through. She pulled it tight behind her, hearing a furious roar from the other side as it closed.

Coral swam breathlessly into the

hallway, into safety.

'Oh, Fabulous, I don't know what to say. You saved me.'

She glanced down to where her little friend had been sheltering under her arm. But Fabulous was not there.

'Fabulous?' Coral looked around frantically. 'Fabulous, where are you?!'

CHAPTER 9
Dr Sweetlips

What had happened to Fabulous? Coral was panic-stricken. Was her friend trapped with those monsters in the kitchen? She couldn't bear it.

Then Coral saw her. The little fish was lying on the floor of the hallway, her eyes closed.

'Fabulous!' cried Coral.

She swam down. She could see one of the spines from the urchins sticking out from under the little fish's fin.

'Oh no! Fabulous, no!' Coral sobbed.

Fabulous was taking short, shallow breaths. She opened one eye and smiled weakly at

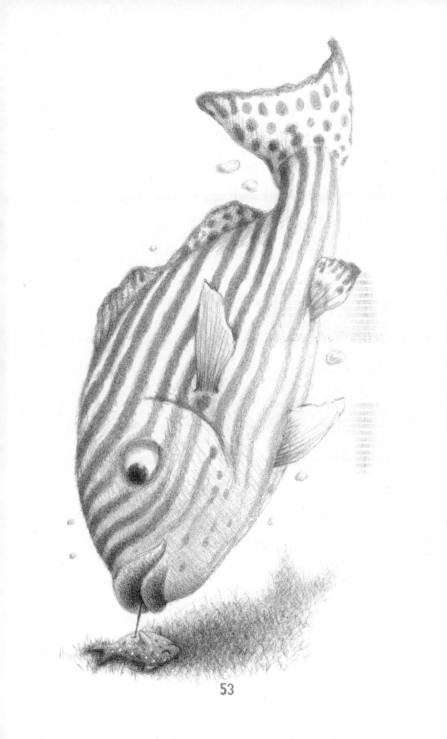

Coral, blowing her a tiny bubble. It was all she could manage.

'Move aside.' It was Ramone. He scooped Fabulous up, and looked closely at the injury.

'Please say she'll be all right, Ramone?' whispered Coral.

'This is one very brave little fish.' He called out, 'Dr Sweetlips!'

A large round fish with fluttering fins swam quickly towards them. He had bulging eyes and an enormous pair of rubbery, pouting lips.

'Fabulous needs your help, doctor. Urgently.'

Dr Sweetlips had a good look at Fabulous. He puckered up his mouth and began pecking at the urchin spine, sucking it out, bit by bit.

Ramone and Coral looked on anxiously. The other fish gathered round too, all waiting in worried silence. After a few minutes, the doctor looked up at Coral. He smiled a gargantuan grin.

'She's going to be just fine!'

Coral felt a huge surge of relief, and fear. Her beautiful little friend could have died saving her. It was almost too much to bear.

'Oh, thank goodness.' She bent down close and gave Fabulous the lightest of kisses. 'Thank you, my little friend. You saved my life.'

Fabulous smiled and blew Coral a minuscule bubble.

'She just needs some rest and, knowing Fabulous, quite a bit of fuss and attention,' winked Dr Sweetlips. 'I'm just glad... Hold your seahorses! Coral, look at the state of you!'

Coral looked down and saw she too had dozens of scratches and urchin spikes buried in her arms and legs. She had been so worried about Fabulous, she hadn't even noticed. Dr Sweetlips began sucking out the spines. Coral winced in pain.

'How did Fabulous know I had...?' Coral's

voice trailed off, ashamed that she hadn't told Ramone where she was going.

'When you didn't come back to the party, Fabulous suspected the worst. She squeezed through the keyhole of the kitchen door and got there just in time.'

'I'm so sorry, Ramone.'

The turtle shook his head, jangling his collection of shell chains, then looked softly at her.

'Nooooooo, Coral. But it's time that you knew the full story.'

CHAPTER 10
Stealth

With Fabulous cupped in one of his fins, Ramone swam back into the living room. Coral followed him, her legs and arms still stinging from the urchins' attack. They settled on the bright orange and lime sofa and the sea creatures crowded in, all shaken by the near escape. Dobbin and Swish linked their tails tightly. Bubba the puffer was on edge, puffed to his fullest, just in case. Otto was trying to calm the Crevettes, who were twittering nervously, and Marvin the eel was quivering like a jelly.

Coral looked at Fabulous and bit her lip. Ramone shook his head, jangling his shells.

'I'm bad, Coral! Baaaad turtle! Should've told ya, should've warned ya! Baaaaad, bad turtle!'

'Warned me of what?'

The old turtle sighed heavily. 'Coral, we have a dangerous enemy. There are dark forces here. But hey, I'm thinking, you must be thinking, "Why is my house underwater and what are all these crazy fish doing here?"'

Ramone's loud raucous laugh burst out of him. He shook his head, rattling his necklaces, and clapped her on the back with his fin.

'Um, yeah, well,' she said, 'it had crossed my mind...'

'I bet it has!' He laughed again, shells jangling. But then his smile slowly dropped.

'We arrived, Coral, the night your tears fell. We wanted to make you happy again. The more tears there were, the more of us came.

More of us to make you smile, girl! We love that great big smile of yours!'

Coral couldn't help but smile again.

'We want you to have joy in your heart! We know that's what your parents would want for you, wouldn't they?'

Coral nodded and the great turtle put a fin around her.

'But not all the creatures here want to bring back happiness.'

Coral frowned. The stingray. The stonefish. The urchins.

'Those dudes you met in the kitchen? Well, they are unhappy souls and they hate to see happiness in others. They want to crush hope. They were drawn by your tears too and they want to make this house a world of darkness. They want to drag us all down. Make us like them, or destroy us.'

'No!' said Coral horrified. 'We must be able to

stop them?'

Ramone raised his eyes to hers, now resting his fin on her arm.

'I'm sorry to lay this on you, girl, but it all comes down to you.'

'To me? Why me, Ramone?' She shivered, remembering the fiery eyes of the stingray.

'Now, don't you go worrying. Let me tell you about that stingray. His name is Stealth. He lost his parents, just like you did. But he locked his heart tight shut and vowed never to love or be hurt again. His pain turned to anger and hate. He despises those who can find hope, because he couldn't.'

Ramone's words struck at her heart. Coral knew what the pain was like of losing those you love most in the world. To feel love seeping away. She understood what it meant to look into the blackness. She understood how Stealth had become how he was.

Ramone saw her face cloud over.

'Hey!' He peered into her face. 'You're not like him. No, no, no, no, NO! Not like him at all.'

It was as if Ramone could read her mind.

'But that's why he wants to hurt you. He knows that if he can make you lose hope, the Sea House will be his world of despair.'

'I won't let that happen, Ramone!' Coral meant it with all her heart, but her voice was shaking. The stingray, Stealth, terrified her. She had felt he could see into her soul and now she knew there was a dreadful bond between them.

He knew her parents had died and he knew how desperate it had made her feel, because he had felt that too. Stealth knew about the part of her heart that was

still so deeply, deeply sad.

Despite this wonderful sea world, the death of her parents left a great sadness inside her, and it frightened her to think that Stealth knew it, and would use it to try to overcome her. Worst of all, she didn't know if she was strong enough to fight him.

'Stealth and his Urchin Army are on the rise. Stealth knows he doesn't have much time left before he must strike. He can sense you have been slipping away from him, finding happiness – 'cos we do have a lot of fun, don't we, girl?' Ramone winked.

Coral laughed in spite of herself. 'You guys definitely know how to have fun!'

'Yeah, maaaaaan!' Ramone erupted with laughter again. 'But Coral, it means Stealth knows he needs to make his move. He grabbed his chance today, but I know that overgrown, flappy-winged, rotten, stinking, smelling…'

'Ramone?'

'Ah, yeah, sorry about that, carried away. But that big bad old fish is preparing to strike. We've gotta be ready for him and I'm afraid, girl, in the end, it's your sea house – only you can win it for us all.'

Coral felt sick with terror. A battle? Fight those hideous creatures? How on earth could she ever do that? She lowered her eyes.

Her gaze settled on Fabulous. The courageous fish was sleeping now. Her breathing was light, her delicate eyelids flickered. As Coral watched her friend, who had risked her life to help her, she knew she must, somehow, find the strength inside her, just as Fabulous had. The question was – how?

CHAPTER 11

We Strike Tonight!

'I am surrounded by IDIOTS!' Stealth swung around, stretched out his wings, then thrashed them hard, sending a mighty pulse through the water, knocking over piles of urchins, and sending his gruesome stonefish stooges, Rocky and Edge, tumbling through the room.

'Have those teeny, tiny brains of yours been washed away? Have they been pickled in a little girl's tears?' he mocked.

Rocky and Edge looked at each other, not quite sure whether to laugh with him or not, but Stealth really didn't sound like he was joking. Rocky grimaced. Edge tried an awkward smirk. Neither response calmed Stealth.

'You are no better than PLANKTON, you blobs of spawn!!!' he roared, whooshing round and round with such force he sent the others scattering into the corners of the room.

Stealth stopped suddenly, his back to them. Slowly, he stretched out his gigantic wings and began to rise above the kitchen units, now covered with black slime, rising higher and higher until he was hovering just below the ceiling.

He turned to address his minions. He was seething and his eyes burned as he scanned each and every one of them. He loathed them all, and hated that he needed them for this fight.

'My desperate … friends.' The last word was dragged from his mouth. 'You know that our very existence depends on defeating this human girl.'

The urchins shifted, murmuring and muttering. Rocky and Edge grinned.

'If you want to survive – and I assume you do?' Stealth drawled.

Rocky and Edge nodded hard, their eyes looking as if they might pop out.

'Then she must be ours!' he boomed. 'We will attack. The Urchin Army is undefeatable. We will break out when they least expect it. When they are at their happiest, we will strike. We will destroy them, crush them. And Coral,' he spat out her name, 'will be brought to ME! Her heart, her soul, her spirit will be mine and I will quash them. Then, and only then, will this

house be ours, to rule in darkness forever!'

The room erupted. Rocky and Edge, easily worked into a frenzy, were quite beside themselves, and the sea urchins rolled and swelled in approval.

'There will be no mercy. There will be no escape. There will be no more happiness!'

Stealth retreated into the far corner of the kitchen, near the back door, and turned his back on the savage crowd, signalling his speech was over.

He closed his eyes. Despite the rhetoric, deep inside him, Stealth knew this would be a fight to the death. He was confident, of course he was, he knew Coral was weak. She was desperately missing those parents of hers. It would be easy! And yet … and yet … there was something else. Something that made him uneasy. She must not be allowed to be comforted by those idiotic creatures any longer. Time was running out, he sensed it.

He spun around and rose high once again.

'There is no time to lose! WE STRIKE TONIGHT!'

CHAPTER 12
A Plan

Coral lay floating above her bed, trying to come to terms with everything Ramone had told her.

'Don't worry, Coral.' Fabulous wriggled her way under the door, coming to comfort her friend. She had made a remarkably swift recovery. This was one tough little fish.

'It's hard not to, Fabulous. I just need to try to work this all out...'

The fish swam right up to Coral's face and tilted to one side as she peered deep into her eyes. It was slightly unnerving.

'Not much time for that, Coral. Ramone has called a tactics meeting in the living room. He thinks Stealth is on the warpath, and we need to be prepared.'

'Stealth is ready to attack?' Coral felt sick to her stomach. She couldn't face him yet, it was too soon.

'Don't worry, it's going to be fine,' soothed Fabulous, seeing the fear on her face. To try to distract her, Fabulous spun around and started tickling Coral's nostril with her tail fin. In spite of herself, Coral giggled. It was ridiculously tickly, and made her want to...

'A-A-A-A-ATISHOOOOOOO...'

As she sneezed, hundreds of teeny bubbles shot out of her nose, sending Fabulous shooting backwards. When the pair of them had stopped laughing, Coral looked again at her little friend.

'OK,' said Coral. 'We can do this, right?'

'Yes!' Fabulous somersaulted.

'And do you know what, Fabulous? I want to do something for all of you. Mum and Dad said that doing things for other people makes them happy and makes you happy inside too, so I may just have a little surprise for you at the tactics meeting!'

'FIN–SLAP!' squealed Fabulous, madly waving the most minuscule fin Coral had ever seen. Coral offered the tip of her little finger in return.

Fabulous zipped to all four corners of the room, zoomed up to the ceiling, down to the carpet, whizzed around Coral's head, somersaulted three times and came to a stop in front of her, quivering with excitement.

'And in case you're wondering, Miss Fabulous,' teased Coral, 'I know exactly what I'm going do.'

CHAPTER 13
The Surprise

There wasn't much time for Coral to practise. The creatures were already gathered in the living room, being briefed by Ramone on their battle tactics. He wanted to make sure they were ready, just in case.

Fabulous had spread the word that Coral was planning a special surprise, and as soon as Ramone had finished explaining the plan of attack, as always, he was ready for a party. It was a relief to have something other than the dreaded battle to think about.

'I think she's going to perform for US!' whispered Dobbin the seahorse to Swish, as they bobbed at the foot of the stairs, waiting for her. They both popped a deeper shade of pink with excitement.

The Crevettes – hundreds of them – were chattering wildly.

'What will she do?'

'Will she sing?'

'Will she dance?'

'I don't know!'

'I can't wait!'

'Nor me!'

'Or me!'

'Or me!'

'When will she start?'

'I don't know!'

'Hope it's soon!'

'Wish it was now!'

'And me!'

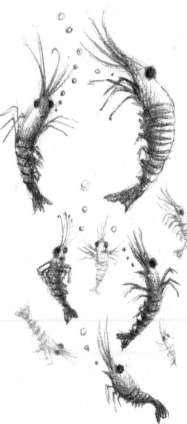

'And me!'

'OOOOOOOOOOHHHHHH!'

Otto the octopus laughed deeply. 'Calm down, Crevettes, all will be revealed soon, I'm sure.'

Marvin the eel was getting excruciating, pre-performance nerves, even though he wasn't performing himself. It's all part and parcel of being in the spotlight, he told himself, but it didn't help.

'My tummy is churning. Oh, I wish she'd start. These nerves are turning me to jelly! Oh, I'm a jellied eel!' he wailed.

'Hey man, no worries!' Ramone gave Marvin a comforting slap on the back, which was actually rather painful. Marvin winced and forced a smile. 'Coral's gonna be just fine, you wait and see.'

⋆

Inside her bedroom, little waves of excitement

were rippling through Coral. She wasn't top of the class, she wasn't the girl who won the prizes at school, but she knew her strengths. She was a pretty cool skateboarder – and she could sing.

Usually, any kind of performance would fill her with dread. She had been in agony if she had to perform in assemblies at school. Standing up in front of hundreds of other pupils and teachers, her heart would beat too fast, her legs would feel weak, the palms of her hands would go clammy, her mouth would be dry. It was always horrible.

'Just try as hard as you can and do your very best, darling,' her mum would say, 'that's all anyone can ever ask of you.'

She would sometimes come home feeling she hadn't done her best, because her nerves had got the better of her. But strangely, she didn't feel scared today. She really wanted to do this.

Coral was as ready as she'd ever be. She opened her bedroom door and the whole house erupted with wild cheering.

She launched herself along the landing carpet, which was super slippery with green slime. Creatures dived out of her way, as she slid faster and faster, pushing with her right leg as if she were riding an invisible skateboard.

As she reached the stairs, she leapt onto the bannisters, kicked into a handstand, and began to slide down the handrail vertically at speed. She'd been building up the courage to try this on her skateboard, but underwater, it was easy! Her balance was perfect! She whizzed down, confident enough to raise one hand and give the crowd a wave. At the bottom of the stairs, Coral tucked up her knees and ended with a double somersault and a bow.

The applause was thunderous! Looking out at the multitude of sea life before her, it suddenly

struck Coral how much her parents would have loved this. For the first time though, she didn't feel that dreadful pain when she thought of them.

She smiled, and just felt love.

CHAPTER 14
Pure Heart

*O*nce again they all gathered in the living room. Coral took a deep breath. She didn't like making speeches, but this felt different.

'Hello, everyone. I … I just wanted to say thank you, actually. Thank you for being my friends. Thank you for…' she swallowed, '…for helping me start to feel happy again. You're like my other family now. A wild, fun, crazy sea family, who I could never have even dreamed of, but I could never have asked for anything more wonderful. So, from the bottom of my heart, thank you.

'I want to share with you a song my dad used to sing to me. It was his favourite hymn. He was from Wales and would sing it in Welsh. It's called *Calon Lân*, which means *Pure Heart*, and I'd like to sing it for you, in the language of my father.'

Coral closed her eyes. She let the memory of her father singing to her wash through her mind, and let the song flow from her heart.

> Nid wy'n gofyn bywyd moethus,
> Aur y byd na'i berlau mân.
> Gofyn wyf am galon hapus
> Calon onest, calon lân.

> *I don't ask for a luxurious life*
> *The world's gold or its fine pearls.*
> *I ask for a happy heart*
> *An honest heart, a pure heart.*

Calon lân yn llawn daioni
Tecach yw na'r lili dlos
Dim ond calon lân all ganu
Canu'r dydd a chanu'r nos.

A pure heart full of goodness
Is fairer than the pretty lily,
None but a pure heart can sing,
Sing in the day and sing in the night.'

Coral's sweet voice, filled with love for her parents and friends, flowed through the entire house. It reached the kitchen. Stealth's eyes narrowed. His great wings shuddered.

'What is THAT?' he snarled, swooping through the room. Although the door was tightly shut, Coral's sweet voice was filling the kitchen.

None but a pure heart can sing,
Sing in the day and sing in the night.

The ghastly gathering braced themselves. Rocky and Edge began cackling uncontrollably, knowing that Stealth was about to explode in fury, although they were finding it difficult not to sway to the music.

'THIS. WAS. NOT. PART. OF. THE. PLAN!' Stealth blasted, whirling his venomous tail as he spun around the kitchen.

Stealth could not bear it. This girl was finding happiness, when she should be pulled into darkness. Well, she would not escape. He had not escaped desolation, and neither would she.

'We attack NOW! Urchin Army! Are you ready for battle?'

Millions of poisonous spikes bristled in anticipation.

'Squadron Stonefish! Ready?'

Hundreds of pairs of eyes blinked blackly from the floor.

'Then let the battle begin! Destroy them all – but remember, Coral must be mine!'

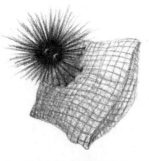

CHAPTER 15

Battle

In the living room, all the sea creatures were hugging each other, deeply moved by Coral's speech and song.

Slowly they became aware of a low, rumbling sound. It was distant at first, but got louder and louder.

Ramone's eyes widened. 'Stealth and the Urchin Army! It has begun!'

Thousands of frightened fish looked desperately at each other.

'It is sooner than we thought, but you are

85

ready, my crew. Be strong, be brave.'

He turned slowly, his shell chains swaying.

'Especially you, Coral.' He smiled his lopsided, beaky grin at her. 'This is it, and I know you can do it, girl.'

Coral was terrified. 'I ... I thought I could, but now...'

'The strength comes from inside you, from that pure heart of yours. Remember that, remember your father's song. Stealth's darkness can never put out that light.'

Coral threw her arms around his enormous, smooth shell, and Ramone wrapped his fins around her. 'We'll always be with you.'

Coral nodded, her throat tightened. She must not cry.

Fabulous shimmered beside her. 'Best friends forever. True friends find a way, right?'

'Right,' Coral whispered.

Fabulous raised a tiny fin for a high five.

Coral put out her finger and brushed it softly along Fabulous's gossamer fin.

'Then let's do this!' bellowed Fabulous in a voice way too big for a fish that small.

At that moment, the doorway of the living room crashed open, and a tsunami of poisonous urchins crashed in.

'ACTION!' Coral and Ramone shouted in unison. Glancing at each other, they nodded determinedly.

'I'll take the hallway,' shouted Fabulous, darting through the black, spiny invaders.

'Sofa!' commanded Coral.

Urchins massed towards them, but hundreds of fish dived behind the sofa, lifting it onto its side, forming a barricade. The sofa fabric was made of woven tweed. It was bold and bright and her mother had loved it, giggling to herself when visitors winced at its garishness.

Now that firm weave was serving as the

perfect trap for the urchin army. As they attacked the sofa, their deadly spines were getting caught in the cushions, trapping them like flies in a web.

'Chairs!' Coral shouted.

The armchairs were transformed into barriers, snaring the urchins as they tried to get past, the strong fabric making it impossible for them to pull away.

Ramone turned ninja with a lamp stand. He swirled it round with his fins, sending urchins scattering with the shade at one end and the wooden base at the other.

Otto the octopus put on the performance

of his life. He used his amazing colour-changing ability to camouflage and attack. Coral saw her mother's yellow curtains come to life as Otto suddenly burst out, sending a tower of menacing urchins tumbling down.

Fighting on the carpet was Marvin the eel, who was crackling with electricity. He zapped urchins by the dozen. The current made their spikes drop out.

The fight seemed to be going in their favour. But Coral understood she must face Stealth, and face him alone. She knew he was waiting for her, and she knew where.

Grabbing hold of a small coffee

table, Coral held it in front of her like a shield and kicked hard. She ploughed through the urchins and headed for the door.

*

Out in the hallway, the battle was raging. Coral saw wave after wave of urchins try to force their way up the stairs. Facing them were the crack team of Sea House defenders.

Fabulous, flanked by the seahorses Dobbin and Swish, yelled orders at a large troop of puffer fish, led by a courageous Bubba.

Every time the urchins made to infiltrate the upstairs, Bubba bellowed, 'PUUUUUUFFFFFFFFFF!"

Rows upon rows of puffers inflated, spikes bristling.

'CHAAAARRRRGGGGEEE!' boomed Fabulous.

As the urchins rose up to attack, the puffers dived from the top of the stairs in defence. Spikes clattered against spines.

The puffers forced the urchins back, stinging them with the venom in their spikes when they could. Then they retreated and resumed their position at the top of the stairs, ready for the next offensive.

Dr Sweetlips was on the landing, tending to any injured puffers. Despite the casualties, they were undeterred. This was a fight to the end.

'Puffers, PREPARE!' shouted Fabulous.

Every uninjured puffer gathered. They had another trick under their fins.

Yet another wave of urchins pushed forward. Bubba was ready.

'Puffers, PUUUUUUUFFFFFFF!'

The puffers puffed, drawing in a huge amount of water into their bodies.

'Puffers, EXPEEEELLLLL!'

All at exactly the same time, the puffers blew out the water with all their might. Together they were like the jet from a powerful garden hose. The urchins plummeted over the bannisters as they were blasted back down the stairs.

Coral's heart swelled with pride. But there was no time to stop. She had to face Stealth. She dodged her way through the mayhem, heading for the kitchen.

Again she saw that strange, greenish glow shining from behind the door. As she approached, the door began to open. Mustering all her courage, Coral swam inside and the door shut hard behind her.

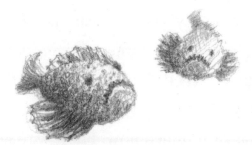

CHAPTER 16
Showdown

It was eerily quiet in the kitchen after the storm of the battle in the hall. Coral blinked hard, trying to adjust her eyes to the ghoulish light. A group of fish were swimming purposefully towards her, teeth bared. Deadly poisonous stonefish. Coral froze. If they all attacked her together, she knew she would not survive.

Her eyes scanned her mother's beloved kitchen. It looked like an ancient shipwreck that had been lying at the bottom of the ocean for hundreds of years. She heard laughter coming from a dark corner of the room. Rocky and Edge emerged from the shadows, their eyes glinting.

She was surrounded now, but it was Stealth she was waiting for. She knew he was here, she could sense him. Coral looked all around her. He was hiding somewhere.

Slowly she lifted her head and looked up at the ceiling. Two great orange eyes, burning like fire, bored into her.

Stealth let out a furious roar. The powerful stingray beat his giant wings, sending a titanic pulse of water at her. She lost her balance, flailing about, as the other creatures just laughed. Desperately she tried to steady herself, but another rush of water tipped her over again. She couldn't stay upright. Every time she righted herself, Stealth beat his wings and she was sent flying. For Rocky, Edge and the other stonefish, it was excellent entertainment.

Coral knew she was getting exhausted. Physically she was no match for Stealth, they both knew that. He was barely even trying. She would have to fight a different way.

'Coward!' she shouted.

The creatures went silent immediately, horrified.

'Come down here and face me! Or are you scared?' she taunted, hoping she sounded bold and fearless. Inside, she was terrified.

The enormous stingray spread his wings out to their fullest. He swooped around with such force, she had to hold onto the now rusty handle of the fridge to stop herself from spinning out across the room.

He came to a sharp halt opposite her, bristling with rage.

'You DARE speak to me like that, you feeble child? You will regret it,' he hissed.

'You may be bigger than me, Stealth, but you will never break me, because I am stronger than you. In my heart I know I am, and you know it too.'

She thought she saw a flicker in his eyes.

Coral had no idea where these words were coming from. But in the kitchen, where there were so many cherished memories of her parents, she knew she was right. Their love would always be with her, and that gave her strength.

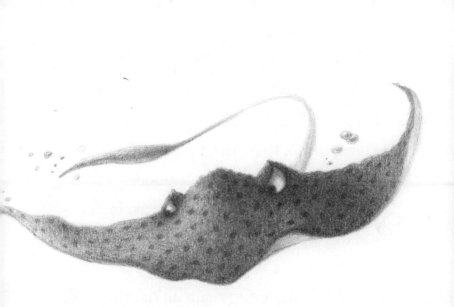

He tried sneering. 'You will never defeat me, Coral. You are weak. Crying, crying, for those dead parents who are GONE! Boo-hoo-hoo,' he mimicked her. 'They're gone forever, do you hear me?'

'Like yours?'

The stingray looked taken aback.

'Yes, Stealth,' Coral spoke slowly. 'I know you lost your parents when you were young, just like me. And I'm sorry.' She paused. 'It doesn't have to be like this for you.'

Stealth was seething. 'You know nothing, you little fool! What about your parents? Do you really think they loved you? If they did, why would they leave you all alone?'

'They didn't leave me. It was an accident!'

'Was it?' snarled Stealth. 'They went swimming to get away from you! They were fed up of you pestering them all the time. They wanted to be free, away from their annoying child. That's why they went into the water that day!'

'No!' Coral choked on the word, holding back her sobs. 'They just wanted to go for a swim together, that's all! It was an accident. They … they didn't know there were rocks… Daddy hit his head. Mummy was trying to save him. It was an accident!'

'If they hadn't wanted to get away from you, they wouldn't have gone, would they? They'd be here today. It's YOUR fault they went swimming. It's YOUR fault they died! If it wasn't for YOU, they'd still be here!'

His words were knives in her heart. Was it her fault? They did get frustrated with her sometimes. Was she to blame?

'No, please…' She sank to the floor, feeling the darkness begin to spread within her.

'Let them go, Coral. They didn't really love you. Join us and find a different kind of happiness. Where there's no pain, no feeling. Join us, Coral.'

The stonefish moved nearer, as she knelt on the floor, rocking gently with her head in her hands. She was desperate and took a deep breath.

'I will...'

An victory smile began to creep over Stealth's face.

'…never give in,' she whispered.

'What. Did. You. Say?' hissed the stingray.

'Never.' She lifted her head. 'I will never join you. Never!'

Stealth roared. He spun around the room, smashing anything in his path, crashing into the table with his venomous tail.

'You will pay the price for this! Stonefish – kill her! But make it slow and make it painful.'

The stonefish circled her, venomous spines bristling. There was no way out. She had failed. She had failed them all – her parents, the sea creatures, everyone.

She felt a sharp jab in her side. Then another in her leg, another in her arm. The stonefish drew back, waiting for the poison to spread. Coral writhed in agonising, intense pain. Another jab in her back, now in her leg.

Her vision was becoming blurry. All she could see were those two fiery eyes burning.

'They're with me...' she whispered, as she

felt them stab her again. 'My parents … my friends … they're with me … in my heart.' She winced in pain. 'Nothing can take them away.'

This feeling of a true, pure love gave Coral one final burst of strength. She hauled herself up and lunged for the door, kicking away the stinging stonefish and shielding herself against the urchins. For a moment she forgot the pain and the poison creeping through her body, and reached out to grab the door handle.

She could hear her mother's words in her head. 'It's the door to the heart of the home, Coral. Keep your home and your heart open.'

'Nobody is keeping this door shut any more!' shouted Coral.

She grasped the doorknob, drew her feet up against the doorframe and pushed back against it with all her remaining strength, wrenching it open, once and for all. Then she swam across the room, the creatures too shocked to stop her, and dragged open the back door as well. Where the power came from, Coral did not know, but as the door opened wide, the sunshine streamed through the house, flooding into the kitchen, shining brightly onto the wretched creatures within, lifting the gloom, bringing light into the heart of the home once again.

It was as if time stood still. She saw her sea friends looking at her in awe from the hallway. Almost in slow motion, she saw the fear on Stealth's face, his crew frozen beside him. She swam purposefully over the threshold of the kitchen and into the hallway, towards her loving friends.

As she did, she felt the last of her strength desert her, and Coral collapsed, sinking down onto the hall floor.

CHAPTER 17
Free

Coral was so weak, she was barely conscious. Everything was a blur. She could feel all the water rushing around her. Coral's tears, which had filled her whole house, were draining away.

She struggled to open her eyes. She saw Stealth, Rocky, Edge, the stonefish and the urchins all being pulled away, out into the sun.

She didn't know if she was alive or dead. For a moment, Coral thought she saw her parents once again. They were looking down at her.

'So brave, my darling,' whispered her mother.

'Proud of you, Coral,' said her father. 'You have a true, pure heart.'

'We'll always love you…'

They began to fade.

Was that Ramone?

'You did it, Coral, girl, you did it. Your strength set us all free. Thank you...'

He was floating away. Otto, Marvin, Bubba, Dobbin and Swish swam in front of her.

'You were so strong, Coral.'

'We're free…'

Coral felt beams of light dancing on her eyelids.

'Fabulous...' she said, opening her eyes, her voice cracking with emotion.

'I love you, Coral,' said the little fish, clearly trying very hard not to cry. 'We'll always be best friends forever, right?' She stroked Coral's cheek gently with her tiny fin.

'Best friends always,' said Coral.

Fabulous blew a stream of perfect, sparkling little bubbles, which gently kissed Coral's face. The glittering image of the fish began to shimmer and fade, and Coral closed her eyes once more.

CHAPTER 18

Friends Forever

When she opened her eyes again, Coral was still lying there on the floor of the hallway. Slowly, she pushed herself up. There was no sign of the magical underwater sea world now. Her house looked as it always had, just a plain, ordinary house. It was silent. She turned around to look at the kitchen. There was no sign of Stealth and his cronies. The doors were wide open.

Had her sea house adventure just been a dream? It seemed almost impossible to believe all that could have happened. Yet Coral knew in her heart it was real, and she would never forget her sea friends. Standing in the empty hallway, Coral felt different. She was stronger now, and ready to begin living again.

She heard a rustling outside the front door and heard a key turn in the lock. It was Aunt Trish, her dad's sister, who had moved into her house with Uncle Jeff to look after her.

Aunt Trish bustled in and stopped abruptly when she saw Coral.

'Oh my darling girl! You're up! Oh, that's wonderful! Just wonderful!' She rushed up and gave Coral the most enormous hug, squeezing her just a little too tightly.

Since her parents died, it hadn't been easy for her uncle and aunt to look after her. She knew Aunt Trish had been very worried. Her aunt peered searchingly into Coral's face.

'How are you, sweetheart?'

'I'm all right, thanks, Aunt Trish. Really.'

She cupped Coral's face in her hands. 'That's my girl,' she whispered, kissing her firmly on the cheek.

'Now. I just popped out to get a few bits from the shop. I wanted to get you some of your favourite snacks. We've got pizza, strawberries, chocolate milkshake, baked beans and popcorn! Oh dear, that all sounds like a very strange mix. Now, did anyone call? Anything happen? Any news? Probably not, nothing very exciting ever happens around here, does it?' She winked.

'Ummm…' Coral didn't quite know what to say.

'Anyway, lovely girl, the big news of the shopping trip is not the pizza or the popcorn.' She took a deep breath.

'I've bought you a little present. I didn't mean to. It was the strangest thing, I had to get it,

I don't know why, I … I just couldn't stop myself, it was…' Aunt Trish trailed off looking slightly confused, then snapped back. 'Anyway, you know I love to treat you, but you see there was this… Oh no you don't! Don't you go making me tell you and spoil the surprise now!'

Coral took a deep breath and smiled. Aunt Trish loved to talk and it was usually quite a while before she got to the point. Aunt Trish would never replace her mum, but Coral loved her and knew she was lucky to have her.

Aunt Trish was still talking. 'Yes, yes, the strangest thing. As I said, wasn't even thinking of presents, but I was on my way out of Bilco's after stocking up. Uncle Jeff and I had parked a little way down the street – in fact, where is he now? Hurry UP, Jeff!' she shouted to Coral's very patient uncle.

'So we were walking down the street, and out of the corner of my eye I saw these little sparkles! Bright blue sparkles! Never seen anything like it in my life! Anyway, the little flashes were coming from the window of … oh! No, nearly gave it away again, didn't I? Come ON, Jeff! Where was I? Oh, yes. I don't know why, but I just had to go in, right there and then, and get it.'

'Coming through!' called Uncle Jeff.

Aunt Trish jumped behind Coral and clapped her hands over her eyes, so she couldn't see Uncle Jeff struggling through the front door and down the hallway carrying something that sounded large and heavy.

Aunt Trish leaned forward and whispered in Coral's ear, 'I hope you like it, darling, I thought it could be a little friend for you.' She sniffed. 'By the way, why does your hair smell…?' She sniffed again. 'Salty?'

Coral smiled.

'Ready!' said Uncle Jeff. 'Come on in, Coral, love!'

Coral shuffled into the living room, past the orange and lime sofa. Aunt Trish tottered behind her on her high heels, hands still clamped firmly over Coral's eyes. Aunt Trish manoeuvred her round for the big reveal.

'Left a bit. No, no, right a bit, a bit more, sweetie. There! Here we go! Are you ready? One, two, three…

TAHHH-DAAAAAHHHH!'

Coral opened her eyes, and stared. She blinked. And blinked again, not quite believing what she was seeing. Her eyes began to fill with tears. But this time, they were not tears of sadness. They were tears of happiness and love and hope.

For there, in the corner of the living room, was a fish tank. And in it, hovering, looking directly at her, was the tiniest, prettiest, most sparkly little fish, twinkling its beautiful bright blue spots, sending flashes around the room.

Aunt Trish and Uncle Jeff were staring at Coral, looking slightly concerned.

'Coral? Coral, are you all right, love? Do you … do you like it?' Uncle Jeff asked nervously.

'Fabulous,' breathed Coral.

'Oh yes!' gushed Aunt Trish. 'Yes it is, isn't it? Just so…'

'No,' said Coral quietly, 'that's her name.'

Coral walked over to the tank. She knelt down and placed her hand up to the glass.

'Isn't it, Fabulous?'

The little fish did a triple somersault and blew a huge stream of bubbles, straight at Coral!

Fabulous's Fantastic Fish Facts

1. I am actually a REAL fish!
It may be hard to believe, but
there are fish as sparkly as me in
the ocean! I am a **Damselfish**.
When we are young, people
often call us Jewelfish, because we
dazzle like diamonds. As I get older,
my glittering spots will start to get smaller and
fade. But I'm always going to shine as brightly
as I can!

2. Seahorses are very romantic.
When they are dating, they
like to dance together, swirling
round and round. It's not the
mum who gives birth to their

babies either. Seahorses are the only species on earth where dads nurture pregnancies and give birth! Wouldn't it be lovely if Dobbin and Swish have a family soon? They have been doing a lot of dancing after all.

3. Sea turtles have been around for a very, very long time. They are some of the oldest creatures on earth. Turtle fossils have been found that are 150 million years old. Dinosaurs became extinct 65 million years ago, so that just shows how old they are! Turtles spend most of their lives at sea, but female sea turtles come ashore to lay their eggs. They look a bit like ping pong balls and turtles can lay as many as 200 at a time! But most of the hatchlings won't survive. It makes me sad to think that nearly all types of sea turtles are under threat of extinction.

4. Puffer fish are not very good swimmers. I feel mean saying this about Bubba and his friends, but most puffer fish are quite slow and clumsy in the water. That's why they puff up! If they can't escape quickly enough from a fish who is trying to eat them, they gulp in large amounts of water and puff up to look big and spiky to scare them away. Those poisonous spines sticking out make puffers really difficult to chew and swallow too.

5. Octopuses DO change colour! Remember when Otto camouflaged himself in the curtains

during the battle in Coral's living room? In the ocean, as well as in Coral's living room, octopuses use this trick to hide from danger. They can change their size, colour, shape and size in a flash! They even shoot out black ink to make the water dark and cloudy so they can swim away from predators without being seen. I would love to be able to do those tricks, wouldn't you?

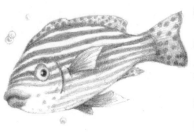

6. Fish can kiss! There are fish with lips like Dr Sweetlips. The **sweetlips** species plant kisses on other fish. Nobody is quite sure why they pucker up, but it's not always friendly. It could be a warning to other fish not to venture into their territory. I'm so glad Dr Sweetlips has such strong lips, because they saved my life!

7. Stingrays aren't bad. Stealth is a very unusual stingray, because most of them in the ocean are actually kind and gentle. It's only when they feel threatened that they will attack with their poisonous tail. Their flattened bodies help them hide in the sand and sometimes they get stepped on accidentally. Then they use their stinger in self-defence. We can't blame them for trying to protect themselves, can we?

8. Eels are very bendy. Remember how Marvin 'Hot Moves' Mackenzie twisted himself into the shapes of letters to spell Coral's name? Well, Marvin could do this because eels have more than a hundred tiny segments in their backbone, called vertebrae. This makes eels very flexible, which is great for busting moves on the dance floor, like Marvin!

9. Stonefish are the most poisonous fish in the world. That's because each has sacks of venom on every one of its 13 spines. But these fish don't often go out of their way to attack. The poison is to defend themselves. Even so, it's no wonder Coral and I were a bit scared of Rocky and Edge at times. Amazingly, stonefish can survive up to 24 hours out of water, when I'd only last a few minutes! Gulp!

10. **Sea urchins**
don't have brains.
Yup, the urchin army
weren't very clever
were they? But sea

urchins can be smart, even without brains.
They have a nervous system that responds
to what is happening around them instead.
And wait for this – the red sea urchin can live
for more than 200 years, which makes them
one of the longest living creatures on earth!

Lucy Owen is a broadcaster and journalist presenting on television and radio for BBC Wales. Lucy hosts the news programme Wales Today and the consumer show X-Ray.

Her first book *Boo-a-bog in the Park* raises money for The Children's Hospital for Wales.

Find out more at **www.lucyowenbooks.com**

Rebecca Harry lives in Cardiff with her two children. She studied Graphic Design in Exeter. From her little studio at home, Rebecca has illustrated picture books for many publishers such as Macmillan, Nosy Crow and Little Tiger Press.

The Sea House is her 40th illustrated book.